The Berenstain Bears
and
MAMA'S NEW JOB

Supper will be a little late —
Love,
mama

When Mama gets home
Too late for a meal,
How will the cubs
And Papa Bear feel?

A FIRST TIME BOOK®

The Berenstain Bears and MAMA'S NEW JOB

Stan & Jan Berenstain

Random House · New York

The Bear family, who lived in the big
tree house down a sunny dirt road deep in Bear
Country, was a very happy family. One of the
reasons was that they were all very *busy*.
Each member of the family had work to do. Papa
Bear cut and split logs and made the wood into
handsome furniture which he was proud to sell.

Mama Bear not only took care of her family, but she managed the whole tree house and tended the vegetable patch as well.

And, of course, Brother and Sister Bear had important jobs too: going to school and keeping up with their schoolwork.

The members of the Bear family had hobbies, too. Papa's favorite hobbies were fishing and napping. He caught almost as many naps as he caught fish. Brother and Sister also had many hobbies. Brother was especially proud of his model airplanes. He liked to have Mama watch him fly his models, and sometimes she helped him fly his tether plane.

Sister was a super rope-jumper and her goal was to jump a thousand times without a miss. She liked to have Mama count for her because Sister could jump faster than she could count.

Since Mama was so busy with her household duties, she had time for just one hobby— but what a hobby! Mama was the best quilt maker in all of Bear Country! Her quilts were light and fluffy, but very warm. Her stitchery was fine and even. And her designs were original and exciting.

Sister Bear slept cozy and warm under a quilt that showed her jumping rope. Brother went to sleep under a handsome airplane design. And the big quilt on Mama and Papa's bed showed the Bear family's beautiful tree house.

HOME SWEET TREE

Yes, the members of the Bear family had happy, busy, full lives. Especially Mama.

"My dear," called Papa to Mama as she worked in the vegetable patch, "if it wouldn't be too much trouble, would you put aside any fishing worms you might find?"

"Look, Mama!" called Brother. "I'm going
to fly my new biplane!"
"I'm going to try for a thousand, Mama!"
said Sister. "Would you please count for me?"

A little *too* full, thought Mama from time to time. She would have liked to have a little more time for her quilts. She had some lovely design ideas she wanted to try:

a sunburst with clouds and bluebirds...

a beautiful bouquet of
flowers with butterflies...

and a harvest scene
with pumpkins and
squash.

But there just never seemed
to be enough time.

Then one day something happened that changed the lives of the Bear family—

something that changed Mama's
quilt-making from a hobby...

into a business!

It might not have happened except for a coincidence, which is when two things happen at the same time.

The two things that happened
were that Papa had a big sale
of some very special furniture,
and on the same day Mama hung
out the family quilts to air.

Folks who came to buy Papa's handsome furniture became excited about Mama's beautiful quilts and wanted to buy them, too. Would-be buyers offered Mama quite a lot of money. They were very disappointed when she told them that the quilts were not for sale.

"With your talent, you really should be in business!" they said.

"Mama in business?" said Papa, patting her on the shoulder. "I don't think so. One business-bear in the family is enough."

But Mama wasn't so sure. She was proud of her quilt-making skills and knowledge. After all, she *was* president of the Bear Country Quilting Club. Other quilt makers often came to her for help and advice.

That evening Papa and the cubs noticed that Mama was very quiet.

She was quiet during supper.

She was quiet during cleanup.

She was quiet all evening. She was quiet because she was thinking—thinking about going into business.

The next day at lunch she made her big announcement.

"I've decided to open up a quilt shop," she said, "and I've rented the empty store just down the road."

"Not that overgrown wreck that's been empty for years!" protested Papa.

"But you don't want to be a business-bear," said Sister. "You're our mama!"

"That's no reason why I shouldn't open my own quilt shop. A lot of mama bears have jobs: Mrs. Grizzle is a sitter; Mrs. Honeybear teaches school; Dr. Gert Grizzly is your pediatrician..."

"Yeah," said Brother, "but they're not our mama!"

"There's really nothing to worry about," said Mama. "Things aren't going to be all that different."

"Will you still count for me when I jump rope?" asked Sister.

"And will you still watch me fly my airplanes?" Brother wanted to know.

"And how about my fishing worms?" asked Papa. "Will you still put them aside for me when you tend the vegetable patch?"

"We'll see about all that," Mama said. "Meanwhile, I have to be at the shop. Some of my quilt club friends are helping me get it ready—and, oh yes," she added as she turned to leave, "there's a lot to do, so supper may be a little late tonight. Ta-ta!"

"Ta-ta," said Papa.
"Ta-ta," said the cubs.

Supper wasn't a little late that night. It was a lot late—and it was Papa and the cubs who prepared it. But they didn't mind, because although Mama was very tired, she was very happy, too—happy and excited! "Guess what!" said Sister as she served Mama her supper. "I reached a thousand jumps today! Brother counted for me!"

"And Sis helped me fly my tether plane! We had a great flight!" added Brother.

"And I weeded the vegetable patch," said Papa, bringing a tub of warm water to Mama for her tired feet.

"Well," said Mama. "I'm very proud of you all."

Papa and the cubs were very proud of her, too. There was no way to tell whether the quilt shop would be a success, but she certainly was giving it a good try.

After about two weeks of hard work, the Bear Country Quilt Shop had its grand opening. It was a very exciting event! Not only did Mama sell her own quilts, but she sold quilts for all the members of her club as well.

It was a great success. Why,
even Mayor and Mrs. Honeypot
came in their long lavender
limousine. They bought one
quilt and ordered three more!

"I know what!" said Mama as she closed up shop that night. "Let's stop off at the Burger Bear for supper! My treat!"

The Bear family celebrated with a delicious Burger Bear supper. Papa and the cubs were very proud of their business-bear wife and mama.

The extra money came in handy too!